DEVON LIBRARIES

Please return/renew this item by the due date.
Renew on tel. 0345 155 1001 or at
www.devonlibraries.org.uk

With thanks
to the following people who
helped make this book possible

David Tubby

Alison Harris, Catherine
Golding, Morton Tooley

David Golding, Tamara Stanton,
Simon Harris,

Suzy Tubby, Craig Halls, Brad Bunyard

Teeny Tiny Witch

By

Sheila Golding

Illustrations by

Colin Rowe

Story by Sheila Golding
Illustrations by Colin Rowe
Edited by Sarah Dawes
Graphic design by Andy Jones
Published by

Blue Poppy Publishing

1st Ed. Hardcover ISBN-13: 978-1-911438-38-0
Paperback ISBN-13: 978-1-911438-39-7

1
Witch Island

Now, let's get one thing quite straight;
Teeny Tiny Witch was no ordinary
witch. She was much smaller than the
other young witches and, though she
tried very hard, she always lacked
something, which made her spells go
wrong. No; Teeny Tiny Witch was not
very good at spells.

Another thing that made her different
was her bright red cloak and hat. She
wasn't very fond of black and refused
to wear it!

Teeny Tiny Witch lived with her mother, and many other witches, on Witch Island. The island was surrounded by the Magic Sea.

In the Magic Sea lived all sorts of strange creatures. There were the two-headed sea python, the large blue sea horse, and many fish-eating plants. The plants looked very pretty but were very, very dangerous. The sea had few fish, as most had been eaten by the plants.

The ruler of this island was Miranda, the icy witch queen. She was named icy because of her cold, evil nature. Everyone on the island was terrified of her.

Fortunately, the queen stayed in her castle most of the time. If ever she was seen, you could be sure that someone was in trouble. BIG TROUBLE!

Teeny Tiny Witch attended the Young Witches' Academy. She had been a pupil there ever since she could remember. Being very small and dressed in red, she was very different to the other, larger young witches who all wore black.

She had started in A.B.1 (Absolute Beginners) class but had never passed to the next level. Every summer there was a final examination. One simple spell had to be completed before the student could move on. Last year, as with all the other years, Teeny Tiny Witch had failed her final exam.

The challenge had been to turn one of your classmates into a frog, and then return her to back to her normal self. Teeny Tiny Witch had picked Lucinda, a promising, clever student, for her challenge.

"KALAZOO, KALAZOO, show a frog, instead of you."

Surprisingly, a frog appeared in Lucinda's place. The other students clapped. Bursting with pride, Teeny Tiny Witch attempted the second part of the challenge. She screwed up her face, waved her arms, and shouted, "KALAZOO, KALAZOO, now bring Lucinda back as new."

Nothing happened. There was a gasp from the other students.

The noise frightened the frog and it quickly hopped away to find shelter. All afternoon, the students searched for Lucinda.

When she was eventually found, hiding under a large water lily leaf, she was carefully captured and taken to see Miss Pillinger, the headmistress.

"WHO DID THIS?" demanded the headmistress.

"It was me," replied a little voice.

The teacher was very angry. She looked down at the little witch in the red cloak and said, "One more chance; just one more. If you don't pass next year, you will be expelled."

Teeny Tiny Witch cried huge tears. Miss Pillinger turned to the frog and whispered special magic words. Lucinda reappeared, but she retained a slight green tint to her skin.

When Teeny Tiny Witch got home, she tearfully told her mother what had happened. Her mother was very kind and offered to give Teeny Tiny Witch extra lessons at home.

2
The Examination

All year, they both worked very hard. Mother thought she noticed some improvement as the summer exams approached.

At last, the day of the final examination arrived.

Teeny Tiny Witch got up, cleaned her teeth, brushed her freshly washed hair, put on her best red cloak and hat and set off for school.

The witches gathered in the playground, waiting for the start of the challenges.

Bazereth was first to go. She sent the school cat flying round the playground but made him land gently at the feet of Miss Pillinger, the headmistress.

It was a free choice examination this year and the other students made horses appear, cats, dogs - and one even managed an elephant!

When it was Teeny Tiny Witch's turn, Miss Pillinger approached.

"I, myself, will be the subject of your challenge," she boomed. "We can't risk harming any more students."

Teeny Tiny Witch's heart sank. 'Not Miss Pillinger,' she thought.

Eventually she pulled herself together and decided to send the headmistress on one small flight around the playground and land back where she started.

"Even you shouldn't mess this up," hissed Miss Pillinger, standing ready.

Teeny Tiny Witch screwed up her face, waved her arms and shouted, "KALAZOO, KALAZOO, fly once round the playground, but come back, do."

Miss Pillinger started off spinning gently around the playground, but the spinning got out of control, going higher and higher.

"Bring her back," yelled the other students, "bring her back!"

Teeny Tiny Witch yelled, "Stop!" at the top of her voice.

The spinning stopped; the crowd gasped. All that could be seen of Miss Pillinger were her thin legs and large feet poking out of the school chimney.

No one in the whole school knew a spell that could release teachers from chimneys, so the fire brigade had to be called!

Miss Pillinger was very, very angry when she was finally rescued and returned to the playground.

Still covered in soot, she dragged Teeny Tiny Witch to her office.

"You failed AGAIN," boomed the headmistress at the small, shaking figure. "Teeny Tiny Witch, you are expelled from this school, forever. You have been given every chance, but you are useless. GO!"

The little witch wandered home in disgrace. Her head hung low as she slowly approached her house.

Mother waited excitedly on the doorstep.

"Did you pass?" she called.

"No," sobbed the little witch. "I was expelled."

Teeny Tiny Witch had just finished her evening meal and had finally stopped crying, when a loud, BANG! BANG! on the door made her jump.

Mother, nervously, opened the door. The icy witch queen stood in the doorway.

Her thin bony features and her sharp manner made her a VERY scary person, indeed. Everyone was afraid of her!

"I understand," boomed the queen, "that your daughter has been expelled from school; is this true?"

"Well, yes but...." began Mother.

"In that case, she will have to leave Witch Island, IMMEDIATELY," the queen snapped.

"Oh, surely not? She's just a child," sobbed Mother.

"IMMEDIATELY," she repeated. "I shall see to it myself. Gather your possessions, child, quickly; I have no time to waste."

Teeny Tiny Witch sobbed and Mother sobbed, too, as Teeny Tiny Witch put a few possessions into a tiny suitcase.

"Here," called Mother, "take George with you; he will look after you for me."

George was Mother's oldest, kindest broomstick who could be relied upon for almost anything.

"Take her a million miles from here and don't come back!" yelled the queen.

Nervously, Teeny Tiny Witch climbed onto George and hung on. Whoosh! Up into the sky they went. When she stopped crying, Teeny Tiny Witch heard muttering.

"A million miles indeed, who does she think I am? I'll be lucky if we make it over the water with my bad back."

Suddenly, Teeny Tiny Witch realized that the muttering came from George.

"I didn't know you could talk," she said.

"Of course I can talk, but sometimes I choose not to. Just hang on. I'll fly as long as I can."

As they flew away, Teeny Tiny Witch took a long, last look at the island that had always been her home.

Big tears rolled down her cheeks, splashing onto George.

"Don't cry, child," said George kindly. "I will take care of you; it will be fun!"

3

Quanga

Teeny Tiny Witch and George flew over the sea, away from Witch Island. It started to rain: pitter-patter, pitter-patter.

The rain got heavier and heavier until it was a drenching downpour. Teeny Tiny Witch had had enough.

"KALAZOO, KALAZOO, make the rain stop; please, please do!"

As if by magic (which of course it was) not another drop fell. She smiled smugly to herself.

Unfortunately, her spell did not stop the thunder.

BANG! CRASH! BANG! RUMBLE!

"What was that?" shrieked Teeny Tiny Witch. She let go of George to put her hands over her ears, which proved to be a BIG mistake.

A strong gust of wind blew her off balance. SPLASH! Into the sea she went.

PLOP! George fell beside her.

CRACKLE, CRACKLE!

Lightning flashed across the sky. The sea was rough and so very cold; the thunder rumbled loudly and the lightning was as bad as ever.

"You and your spells!" said George. "Just swim!"

Teeny Tiny Witch said, "Oh George, I'm terribly sorry."

She swam, with George tucked under one arm.

On and on she swam, getting colder and more uncomfortable and very, very tired.

After an hour of paddling through choppy waves, George said, "Look!"

Teeny Tiny Witch saw an island just ahead and she sighed with relief.

She was exhausted, but the sight of land renewed her hopes. She still shivered and shuddered, but she kept going.

Finally, they reached the island.

She grabbed at an old tree root, took a deep breath, and scrambled up the bank onto the island.

An icy wind blew across the shore. It was much, much colder here than on Witch Island.

"We need to find shelter," said George.

They looked around. Nearby, they saw an entrance to a cave. The bitter wind blew even stronger, so they hurried inside.

Sitting on the floor of the cave, Teeny Tiny Witch and George were still cold.

"Brr," shivered George. A shaking broom was a strange sight, even to Teeny Tiny Witch. It made her feel very sorry for her friend, so she thought about how to warm him up.

After a few minutes, Teeny Tiny Witch had an idea. "We need a fire," she said, "but there is nothing here that will burn."

George, still shivering, said, "Well, don't look at me. I know I'm made of wood, but I'm your way out of here. Although I can't fly now; I'm too wet. See how swollen with water my bristles are?" he moaned.

Teeny Tiny Witch said, "Oh, no, I would never even think of using you for firewood. There's just one thing to do."

Braving the storm, she went outside, gathered an armful of twigs and brought them into the cave.

"KALAZOO, KALAZOO, make a fire to warm us through."

Well, the twigs started to dance around the cave, but not one of them showed any signs of fire. "Oh, no, this won't do at all," Teeny Tiny Witch cried out.

"Maybe I can help?" A little voice spoke from the back of the cave.

Teeny Tiny Witch jumped, almost losing her red hat. She looked around in surprise, for she had thought they were alone.

George jumped too, and cried out in pain as he hurt his back again.

Two red glowing lights approached. As the lights got closer, the owner of the lights came into view.

A small, green, scaly face appeared, with two large brown eyes, and glowing nostrils, the source of those red lights.

"It's a d-dragon," stuttered Teeny Tiny Witch.

"I-I know," stuttered George.

"I'm Quanga," said the dragon. "Don't be scared. I'll light your fire for you." The little dragon, who was only a baby really, pushed the twigs together. He took a deep breath and blew.

Maybe you didn't know, but dragons, even baby ones, breathe out fire. The twigs started burning and soon everyone was warm.

As they huddled close to the fire, Quanga kept looking worriedly towards the entrance of the cave.

"What's wrong?" asked Teeny Tiny Witch.

"It's Mother; she should have been back by now. She left me here earlier, but that was hours ago."

"Your m-mother?" Teeny Tiny Witch looked terrified.

4
Duchess

"Is your mother big?"

"Very big," replied Quanga, "but she's kind and good. She won't hurt you."

"Where has she gone?" enquired George.

"She's at work again," said Quanga sadly. "She works for the terrible wizard, keeping his castle warm, and making sure all the fires behave themselves. He hates to be cold. But he won't allow me there, because he says I distract Mother from her work and he doesn't want me under foot. She doesn't like leaving me in the cave, but she told me to stay hidden. I didn't know you would come in and then be so miserably wet. How did you get so wet, anyway?"

"We fell in the sea and then swam until we found this island. The terrible wizard? Who is he? And why is he called terrible?" asked Teeny Tiny Witch.

"He rules the island," said Quanga. "He used to be good and kind, but just lately... he is so clumsy, he doesn't care who he bumps into or steps on. He yells in a bad-tempered way. Everyone keeps away from him, if they can!"

"Well, you are probably better off here," said George, who was now dry and feeling lots better. "Thanks for this fire; my bad back barely hurts, now."

"You are welcome. So tell me, where you come from, are there dragons?"

Teeny Tiny Witch and George told Quanga about home and, as it got later, they decided to take naps, saying he should not worry because his mother would probably be there when he woke up next morning.

Quanga sighed, "I hope so; I miss her, terribly."

The three friends chatted for a while, and then gradually, one by one, they fell asleep, curled up together on the floor of the cave.

Morning came. The sunlight streamed in through the entrance, and they all woke up.

Quanga looked around sadly. "She's still not here. She's never gone for this long; something must be wrong." Big tears splashed down his little face.

"We'll go and look for her," said George kindly.

"Do you know the way to the castle?" asked Teeny Tiny Witch.

"Oh, yes, I think so," Quanga said eagerly. "Let's go, NOW."

The three friends set out. George floated along beside Teeny Tiny Witch, who refused to ride him if she could walk.

They followed a little path for a while, but then snowflakes started falling. Faster and faster they fell.

Teeny Tiny Witch, soon up to her armpits in snow, listened as George complained about the cold on his back.

Quanga stopped and scooped them both up. "Ride my back," he said. "We will go much faster. I was worried about Mother or I would have offered sooner."

So they rode on his back and, to make the path easier to travel on, Quanga took deep breaths, so that when he breathed out, the fiery air cleared the pathway.

On and on they went and the snow continued falling. It became deeper and deeper, but at last they saw a castle towering high above them.

"Is that it?" asked George. "Yes, it is," replied Quanga, nervously.

They approached the castle as fast as they could, but Quanga confessed he wasn't sure the wizard would be happy to see them.

"I just realized we don't know your mother's name," George said.

"It's Duchess," replied Quanga.

"That's a funny name for a dragon," Teeny Tiny Witch laughed, and then apologized. "Oh, I'm sorry. I didn't mean to be rude."

They all called out, "Duchess, Duchess, where are you?"

They crossed the bridge of the castle, and approached the huge door. Quanga grabbed the heavy brass door knocker with his teeth and knocked.

Pretty soon, a large dragon appeared in the doorway. She had even larger eyes than Quanga, and huge fiery nostrils. Quanga was so relieved to see his mother. He rushed forward, and his passengers almost fell off.

5

The Terrible Wizard

"Sorry I didn't come back home last night," said Duchess, giving Quanga a hug, "but the wizard has had an accident. He can't move and I've been keeping him warm all night. Come in, come in! I've been worrying about you, all alone in the cave. But I see you have some friends with you?"

"This is George and Teeny Tiny Witch, Mother."

They all said hello.

Duchess explained, "The terrible wizard toppled down the stairs, just as

I was about to leave. He couldn't get up and told me not to lift him. He was such a pitiful sight, and begged me not to leave him."

From the foot of the stairs, the terrible wizard cried out, "Duchess, come back; who is that and can they do magic? Maybe with magic, I can get back on my feet."

Teeny Tiny Witch stepped forward.

"Hello, I can do magic," she spoke out bravely, but added, "I can't say how it will turn out though."

"Do it! Just do it! I order you, now, Teeny Tiny Witch."

Teeny Tiny Witch screwed up her face and shouted, "KALAZOO, KALAZOO, rise up wizard, rise up do."

The wizard flew upwards.

"That's enough," called out a worried George.

The wizard started to spin around the huge hallway, narrowly missing a large chandelier. Up the winding staircase went the wizard. "Help!" he cried, "don't let me fall again."

"STOP!" yelled Teeny Tiny Witch. "Marshmallow pillow landing!" she added.

The wizard dropped like a stone, and then he bumped and banged down every stair but was cushioned on giant, puffy, marshmallows, which tossed him high before he bounced to the next one.

"Ouch, that hurt," he shouted, when an elbow banged the stone wall. Finally he came to rest at the bottom and Teeny Tiny Witch and Quanga gave him a hand back onto his feet.

"Not bad, little Miss," the terrible wizard said. "That was smart thinking." He didn't sound so terrible, after all.

All this time, George, who was quite a clever broomstick, had been thinking, 'He bumps into things, steps on things and fell downstairs last night.'

He decided to be bold, and said to the wizard, "I think I know your problem." "You do?" said the wizard, a large smile appearing on his face. "What is it? Oh, please, tell me!"

"I think you need glasses."

"Right," said Teeny Tiny Witch "KAL...."

"NO," said George firmly, "we've had quite enough of your spells for today."

"I know where to get glasses; I'll go now," Duchess said. "If you will stay here with the wizard, I will go and get him a pair. There is a store nearby called The Good Elf store. It sells absolutely everything."

"By all means, buy the best pair you can find. And hurry; my eyes and limbs can't take much more of this," said the wizard.

Then, with a bit of help from George, he made them all a hot drink. By the time they had finished, Duchess was back.

She carefully carried three pairs of glasses. One by one, she helped the wizard try them on.

When they came to the last pair, a huge smile spread across the wizard's face. "I can see so much better. Things have been a blur for so long. This is GREAT!"

He danced all around, bragging about all the detail he saw.

"Oh, I know just what I want to do!" he said, clapping his hands together. "Duchess, you have earned a day off. Go home and get some rest. I will be fine."

Duchess, Quanga, Teeny Tiny Witch and George left the wizard admiring his new glasses in the mirror.

A few days later, Duchess came home with a puzzled expression. When they asked her if there was something wrong with the wizard, she laughed. "The wizard doesn't have time to be terrible any more. He is too busy with his new hobby: EMBROIDERY!"

6
Cooking With Duchess

Teeny Tiny Witch and George had quite settled into cave life. The two dragons had welcomed them into their home and life was good.

Duchess still went to work at the wizard's castle, but Quanga didn't mind too much now that he had company.

One evening, Duchess rushed into the cave. Her nostrils were flared and bright red. She was quite out of breath.

"Good news, good news," she panted, "we all have a job tomorrow."

Teeny Tiny Witch, George and Quanga weren't quite as excited as Duchess at the thought of a hard day's work.

"What do we have to do?" enquired George at last.

"Cooking; it's cooking," replied Duchess, who was hardly able to contain her excitement.

"Oh," said Teeny Tiny Witch; she hated cooking.

They all groaned at the news, but Duchess didn't even notice. She was humming contentedly and searching around in her cupboard looking for the perfect pot to make some potato soup for supper.

"Come and help me so you can get some practice," she demanded.

Quanga, George and Teeny Tiny Witch all did as she said, because Duchess was not someone you said no to! However, as they worked, they began having fun, and supper was quite delicious.

Later George said, "It's much more fun when you share the work, and the food tastes ten times better."

Quanga and Teeny Tiny Witch totally agreed and so they went to bed looking forward to the next day.

Morning came, and Duchess ushered them all out of the cave. She explained, "The wizard is having a tea party. His cousin is coming and he hasn't seen her for ages, but he needs help to make the cakes and jellies."

Teeny Tiny Witch still didn't like cooking, but she cheered up at the news. Cakes and jellies sounded a lot more exciting to make.

"We need to get the ingredients on the way, so we will stop in at the Good Elf Store," Duchess added.

When they arrived at the shop Duchess bought flour, sugar, butter, eggs and jelly.

Quanga saw a large box of chocolate biscuits and a box of icing sugar. "May we have these as well?" he asked.

"OK," said Duchess.

"And these?" asked Teeny Tiny Witch, picking up a jar of sprinkles.

"Yes," said Duchess, "but that's all."

Teeny Tiny Witch carried the sprinkles up to the counter where a red-headed elf with a pointed nose and very heavy eyebrows waited to serve them.

As she waited for the others to put the items on the counter, Teeny Tiny Witch carefully examined the label on the sprinkles. It read, 'These are magic, take extra care how you use them.' This was in small letters at the bottom of the label and she wondered just what that meant. She put the sprinkles up on the counter and Duchess paid with three gold coins.

They gathered all the items they had bought and left the store, in good spirits and looking forward to making desserts for the party.

Quanga said, "Thank you, Mother, for including us; this will be lots of fun."

The others added their thanks, too, which pleased Duchess who said, "If the wizard will allow us, we will all be at the party as guests, so try not to get too messy."

"Oh, we will be very careful," Quanga said, and Teeny Tiny Witch nodded, although she was still wondering if she should have got those magic sprinkles.

George told her not to worry.

"I will sweep everything up in a jiffy and dust off all of you too, if it's needed," he told them.

7
The Wizard's Tea Party

When they arrived at the castle, Duchess and her helpers were greeted by the wizard.

"Come in, come in," he called. "We need to make everything perfect. Last time my cousin Miranda came to tea, she found fault with EVERYTHING. This time I want it all to be so good that she can't complain."

"We'll do our best," said Duchess as she set about making a sponge cake. In went the butter and sugar.

Duchess mixed them well before adding the eggs and then the flour. After stirring it all together, Duchess was pleased with her efforts and popped the mixture into the oven.

Meanwhile, George and the wizard had made lots and lots of red jellies.

Quanga was going to put the cream on the jellies when they were set; Teeny Tiny Witch had the job of icing the cake.

They both waited eagerly to do their bit towards the tea party.

The jellies were ready and Quanga put a neat blob of cream on the top of each one.

He carried them into the dining room and carefully placed the tray of jellies onto the elaborate table.

Teeny Tiny Witch was getting anxious; the cake seemed to take forever to cool; and then the doorbell rang.

DING, DONG! DING, DONG!

The wizard rushed to answer the door.

"Come in, Miranda; we have a lovely tea prepared."

"It'd better be, last time was a disaster," replied his guest, in an icy voice.

As soon as Teeny Tiny Witch heard her speak, her face fell.

"No, it can't be! Anyone but her!" she moaned.

Miranda, or the icy witch queen as Teeny Tiny Witch knew her, strutted up the hall and into the dining room.

"Is it ready?" she demanded.

Teeny Tiny Witch panicked. She swung her wand and tried a speed up spell.

"KALAZOO, KALAZOO, ice the cake and be quick, too."

Soon the cake was covered with a thick, even layer of icing. It looked very nice.

'Oh! That went well,' she thought. 'But I forgot the sprinkles. I'd better be careful with these, though.' She remembered the warning on the label.

"KALAZOO, KALAZOO, put on sprinkles, but just a few."

The sprinkles jar jumped off the shelf and did a little jig in mid-air above the cake. It tilted over as the sprinkles flew out and began covering the icing.

"That's enough," said Teeny Tiny Witch.

The sprinkles jar took absolutely NO notice and carried on shaking sprinkles onto the cake, only stopping when it was completely empty.

'Oh, dear,' thought Teeny Tiny Witch, 'will this do?' She was near to tears, for she wanted to do well in front of the icy witch queen.

She bit her lip as Duchess came in to collect the cake. Seeing her upset, Duchess asked her what the matter was.

Teeny Tiny Witch quickly told Duchess about how Miranda was the icy witch queen and how she had made her leave Witch Island, after failing her exams.

Duchess said, "That doesn't seem fair, dear. I will take care she doesn't see you."

She hid Teeny Tiny Witch in the large pocket of her cookery apron. "She won't spot you in there," smiled Duchess.

8
The Icy Witch Queen

Sitting around the table were the wizard, the icy witch queen, Duchess (with Teeny Tiny Witch in her pocket) and Quanga. George stood in a dark corner of the room so that he wasn't seen.

"Well, that cake *does* look *delicious*," commented the icy witch queen.

Picking up a large silver knife, she approached the cake.

She leaned over eagerly.

With a swift downward movement, she sliced the... TABLE.

"Miranda!" said the wizard, "what *are* you doing?"

"That cake moved!" shrieked Miranda.

"Cakes don't move, silly," laughed the wizard. "Try again."

The icy witch queen picked up the silver knife, and with a very determined look on her face, again she sliced down on... the TABLE.

"There, did you see it? It moved; I'm telling you, it MOVED," she shouted.

The wizard was fumbling for his glasses. "Maybe YOU need these more than I do," he laughed.

"I do NOT need glasses," barked the queen.

All this time, Quanga, Duchess and Teeny Tiny Witch (who was peeping out of Duchess's pocket) could see the cake moving and thought it hilarious! They were doing their best not to laugh as the queen tried again.

"Hold the cake," she commanded.

"Very well," said the wizard and grabbed at the tray to hold it steady while his cousin sliced the cake.

At least, he tried to hold it steady. It started spinning rapidly in the middle of the table, and there was no way he could hold on. He lost his grip and flew right into Duchess's lap.

He looked up, with his glasses on sideways and said, "Thanks for the catch."

Duchess said, "I didn't catch you; it was a lucky landing."

The cake was still spinning like a top, but something unusual was taking place... it was growing fat little arms and legs which seemed to be waving and kicking as the spinning was slowing down.

When it stopped spinning, it had changed. It now had a grumpy face.

The cake saw the red jellies and started scooping them up and throwing handfuls at the icy witch queen.

"How DARE you?" she screamed.

The cake took no notice; it continued to pelt her with handfuls of sticky red jelly.

The queen had jelly in her hair and all over her face, and she had cream up her nose. Everyone started laughing.

The icy witch queen angrily got up from the table and headed for the door.

"Never will I come back here," she shouted, "NEVER!"

The cake jumped from the table, armed with bowls of jelly, and the icy witch queen ran away screaming. It chased her down the path, away from the castle, covering her with sticky jelly as she ran.

The wizard pointed and laughed. He laughed so hard he was holding his sides.

Duchess was embarrassed, and apologized. "I'm SO sorry," she said, "my cake ruined your tea party."

Teeny Tiny Witch stood up and said, "No, Duchess; that was my fault. Those sprinkles were magic."

"Don't be sorry," chuckled the wizard, "today couldn't have been any better; it taught Miranda that even SHE can't get her own way ALL the time and, even better, we still have a large box of chocolate biscuits to enjoy!"

So they all sat down and had a wonderful tea party, laughing about the icy witch queen being pelted with sticky jelly by a magic cake with fat legs. The wizard laughed so hard he had to wipe his glasses with the tablecloth.

"I've never laughed so much in a hundred years. Thank you, Teeny Tiny Witch."

Teeny Tiny Witch blushed as red as her red cloak and hat.

Soon everyone was laughing, having a great time, eating chocolate biscuits with their tea.

"Would you show me some of your magic tricks?" Teeny Tiny Witch asked the wizard. She was impressed by him and excited at the thought of watching him perform. She hoped she might learn something useful.

Normally, wizards are real show-offs, pleased to impress anyone willing to watch, so she was quite shocked when he said, "No."

"Please," she pleaded, hopefully.

"I-I can't," his face fell, "not since my wand was stolen; my beautiful, shiny, gold wand that my grandmother gave me. I've had it since I was a child. Without it, I am a completely useless wizard. I can't do any magic, not any more. I would like to be on my own now, so excuse me, but please, go home, all of you."

9

Lucinda

"I feel terrible," Teeny Tiny Witch told Duchess as they walked back to the cave. "I had no idea the wizard's wand had been stolen. I didn't mean to upset him."

"It's not your fault, child. You weren't to know," Duchess said kindly.

"But who would steal the wizard's wand?" asked Teeny Tiny Witch.

"No one knows who did it and it has not responded to his magical returning spell, so that makes him feel sure he has lost his powers. However, I do have my suspicions," replied Duchess. "I think Miranda, the icy witch queen, did this. She was always jealous of the wizard, always complaining that she should be the centre of attention and that it is she who knows the most powerful magic in the land."

"Maybe we could get it back for him?" Teeny Tiny Witch's mind was working overtime.

"You? Go up against the icy witch queen? I don't think so," Duchess said, concerned.

Then Quanga cried out, "What's that?" His sharp eyes saw something high in the sky, flying towards them. "That's not a bird or a dragon," he said.

Whatever it was, it landed just over the top of the next hill.

Teeny Tiny Witch, Duchess and Quanga raced up the hill. They got to the top and peered over it, cautiously.

"That looks like Lucinda," said Teeny Tiny Witch, noticing the pale green face of the young witch that had just landed. It seemed such a long time since they had last seen each other in the Young Witches' Academy.

"Lucinda! Lucinda!" she called. "Hello, how did you find me?"

Lucinda rushed over, carrying Henry, her new broomstick. They hugged each other, and Teeny Tiny Witch was so happy she cried.

"It's good to see you," Lucinda said. "I have so much to tell you!"

They walked back to the cave, where the two friends chatted long into the night. By the end of it, Teeny Tiny Witch could hardly believe all that had happened on Witch Island since she had left.

Lucinda told her that the icy witch queen had never returned from the tea party at the wizard's castle. No one had seen or heard from her since.

She also told her about Peggaty, who had joined the academy not long after Teeny Tiny Witch had left.

Peggaty was not nice at all, and treated everyone as though they were below her, insisting they should do what she said. If they refused she put a spell on them; several of the girls had been turned into balls to be kicked around, or balloons that Peggaty had left to float away.

She was a terror, and nobody could control her. And with the icy witch queen gone, there was no one there to punish her for her bad deeds.

She was a large witch for her age and Miss Pillinger was powerless to control her.

"Peggaty knows very, very deep magic," said Lucinda, "even more than Miss Pillinger. She lived with the icy witch queen, but now that she is gone, Peggaty stays at the castle alone. There are lights on all evening and loud music blasting way into the night.

"Peggaty is dangerous. When she looks at you, she scans your mind. It feels as though she knows what you are going to do, before you know yourself.

"She brought a plague of huge spiders - horrible creatures - into the academy. Poor Miss Pillinger jumped onto her desk to escape them.

"Hailstones, as big as footballs, have fallen from the sky. Worst yet, all the plants in the Magic Sea have died. The blue sea horse escaped with his family. Ned-Ted, the two-headed sea python, has only himself to talk to; he is so bored and lonely. Oh, it's terrible."

Lucinda cried as fat teardrops trickled down her cheeks.

"What can we do?" asked Teeny Tiny Witch.

"I'm hoping that you can help," said Lucinda. "Miss Pillinger sent me to find you. She was told by the Magic Mirror that you are our last hope. She didn't believe it until it had told her three times, but then she said it must be true."

"Well I still don't believe it. Me? Witch Island's last hope?" Teeny Tiny Witch shook her head.

"She insisted that you must come home right away," said Lucinda. "She said I can't return alone. Please come; I don't want to be banished because I couldn't persuade you to return with me," she sobbed.

"But how can I help?" Teeny Tiny Witch was surprised that anyone would even think of asking her.

"Well, Peggaty doesn't know you, and you're very small. Maybe Peggaty won't see you until it's too late. We must think of a plan. Are you willing to come back to Witch Island and give it a try?" Lucinda looked hopeful, through her tears.

"Of course," said Teeny Tiny Witch, feeling delighted at the thought of going home again. "I can see Mother, too, can't I? I've missed her so much."

"Yes, yes," agreed Lucinda. "Come now, we must leave soon."

They hurriedly told George and Duchess about the plan to go back to Witch Island.

"I will come with you," Duchess said. "I will fly you both back to the island. Please, George, will you stay and keep an eye on Quanga and the wizard?"

"I'll be glad to do so," said George. "Be careful, all of you."

10
Return to
Witch Island

The journey back to Witch Island passed more quickly than Teeny Tiny Witch had expected. Riding on Duchess's back was fun. Lucinda sped along beside them on Henry.

After what seemed only a short time, Teeny Tiny Witch saw Witch Island in the distance. A wide, happy smile spread across her face. "Home," she said. "Home at last."

Soon, they were close enough to see the island's shore.

"Oh my, there she is! That's Peggaty and she's got Ned-Ted there too. She's shouting at him. That poor python." Lucinda shook her head.

"Oh, she's awful. What should we do?" Teeny Tiny Witch asked.

"We will land on the beach, nearby but out of sight. Be very quiet, for we must not let them know we are back yet," said Lucinda, as they carefully circled around for a landing.

As they flew by, Teeny Tiny Witch stared at the teenage witch, with Ned-Ted, the two-headed sea python in front of her. Both his heads were drooping down and he looked so sad. That made Teeny Tiny Witch very upset. She hated bullies. Peggaty needed to be taught a lesson!

They landed behind some prickly bushes, in a clearing overlooking the shore.

Duchess, Teeny Tiny Witch and Lucinda, carrying Henry in her hand, all crept closer to Peggaty and Ned-Ted.

"I killed the plants and I can just as easily kill you," the bully was shouting, "so you had better be nice to me, and show some respect."

They could hear Ned-Ted sobbing, but she went on shouting at him.

"Oh, don't be such a cry baby! You call yourself a two-headed python? You're nothing but a two-headed worm. I'll be back in thirty minutes and you'd better have that fish for me, because I want fish for my dinner. Or would YOU rather be my dinner? Python might just be very tasty." Peggaty smacked her big lips and laughed loud and long, as she stomped off toward her castle home.

Teeny Tiny Witch and the others exchanged worried looks.

The sobbing noises grew louder, and Teeny Tiny Witch couldn't bear it any longer.

She stepped out of hiding.

"Is someone crying?"

Ned-Ted looked around, very scared, but when he saw who it was both his faces lit up, hopefully.

"Oh, my, it's Teeny Tiny Witch! It's been so long since we last saw you. Oh, dear friend, a terror has taken over the island," Ted said. "Who is that with you?" He stared at the bushes.

At this, Duchess appeared, and the python gasped, "A dragon? Oh my!" He backed away.

"Hello," Duchess said, "Don't be alarmed, we're your friends. What's wrong?"

With tears still rolling his faces, Ned-Ted said, "Oh, there you are, Lucinda and Henry. It's so good to see you all again, and to meet you, too, Duchess. Maybe you could make toast of that hateful Peggaty."

Between sobs, Ned continued, "She wants us to give her a fish for her dinner. She knows all the fish are gone. There aren't any fish."

"What to do? She means to eat US and we believe she will, too. She's worse than an ogre," Ted said.

"She said if there was no fish for her, I'd be sorry." Ned-Ted said together.

"Well, just leave it to me," said Teeny Tiny Witch. "She doesn't know about me and I'm angry now. She's done a lot of mean things. It's time to get even."

"Oh, please be careful," Lucinda begged, and the others nodded.

"If I need help, just back me up," said the brave little witch.

"We will," they promised.

A noise from the direction of the castle warned them that someone was coming. THUD! THUD! THUD! It was Peggaty! She called out, "Got my fish yet?"

Ned-Ted quivered as his heads bobbed lower and lower. "Peggaty's coming back for her lunch," he groaned.

Teeny Tiny Witch and her friends hid behind the prickly bushes.

Peggaty marched up to Ned-Ted. "Where's my fish?"

The terrified python trembled and Peggaty smiled. She enjoyed intimidating others. Teeny Tiny Witch frowned.

"I've looked and looked for a fish. There are none left. I'm sorry, Miss Peggaty."

"NO FISH?" boomed Peggaty. "You'll be sorry. I killed the plants and I can just as easily kill you. I want my fish.

I'm hungry and getting angrier by the second," she shouted.

"I've got a fish for you," said a little voice from behind the bushes.

Peggaty looked around, but saw no one. "Who's that speaking? Come out and face me."

"A big juicy fish," the little voice continued.

Duchess came forward. She carefully avoided looking into Peggaty's eyes for fear of being scanned.

"Where's my fish?" demanded Peggaty. "Dragon, or not, I want my fish."

"There is no fish; just a little joke; ha, ha, ha!" Duchess laughed.

Peggaty was furious. "You'll be sorry," she shouted at Duchess.

"I will not," said Duchess, and with her long tail, she batted Peggaty into the prickly bushes.

"Ow, ouch, ow!" Peggaty yelled.

Everyone laughed as hard as they could. Peggaty did not like being laughed at. Furious, she scrambled from the bushes with her fists clenched tightly, gnashing her teeth.

Teeny Tiny Witch jumped out and pointed her wand at Peggaty, calling out a spell, "KALAZOO, KALAZOO, you wish for a fish, and a fish is what I'll turn you into."

Lucinda started to wave her wand, too, just to make sure the spell worked, but Duchess stopped her, with a shake of her head. "Let her do this on her own, dear," she whispered.

There was a flash as Teeny Tiny Witch waved her wand and Peggaty turned into a huge fish, flopping around on the sand and gasping for air. "Help me," she cried, "I can't be a fish; I can't swim. Oh, change me back, please."

"No changing back, sorry," Teeny Tiny Witch said. "Get in the water, and be gone from here."

The big fish wobbled toward the Magic Sea, rolling over and moaning, "I'll die before I get there."

Duchess came up and batted her into the sea with her tail. "There you go," she said.

In the water, Peggaty sank, and then resurfaced. She called out to the friends gathered on the shore, "Oh, help me! I can't swim!"

"Time to learn," they all said together.

Teeny Tiny Witch raised her wand again. "Now to get the fish-eating plants back to the Magic Sea; KALAZOO... "

"Stop," yelled Peggaty, "at least give me a chance to get away."

"Swim then," said Teeny Tiny Witch. "Be gone, fish Peggaty and don't ever return."

"I won't, I won't," gasped Peggaty as she splashed and bobbed in the water. The friends watched as the big fish swam slowly away.

"Now you know how others feel!" called out Ned-Ted, as Peggaty disappeared in the waves.

11
A New Queen

Lucinda wanted to go and tell Miss Pillinger the good news and she set off for the academy, riding Henry to get there as fast as she could. Teeny Tiny Witch wanted to see her mother more than anything else and, with Duchess following, she ran to their cottage, calling out, "Mother, Mother, I'm back!"

Mother was in the herb garden, collecting herbs to dry for spells as well as for cooking.

Teeny Tiny Witch threw her arms around her mother's neck and kissed her cheek over and over again. "Oh Mother, I missed you so much!"

"Darling child," said Mother, giving Teeny Tiny Witch an enormous hug, "I'm very happy to see you."

Then she spotted Duchess and she jumped in alarm. "Oh my, and you have a dragon, too."

"I'm Duchess," said the dragon. "Nice to meet you."

"Hello, I'm Mother Pearl. Teeny Tiny Witch is my daughter."

Teeny Tiny Witch told her mother, "Duchess is good and kind, and her son is my best friend, Quanga. He's with George back at the wizard's island. Oh, I have so much to tell you."

Mother and Teeny Tiny Witch walked into the tiny cottage. Duchess was far too big to fit through the doorway, so she poked her head through an open window.

They were chatting away when a loud knocking came at the door. It was Lucinda, who had returned with Miss Pillinger.

"Come in, come in," said Mother. "Sorry, there's not much room, for our home is very small."

"It's perfectly fine, Mother Pearl," Miss Pillinger said. "Hello, Duchess. Lucinda mentioned you. It's nice to meet you."

Miss Pillinger turned to Teeny Tiny Witch.

"Thank you so much for what you have done for us; we're very grateful for your help in banishing Peggaty."

Miss Pillinger smiled at Duchess, too. "I've brought a large tin of chocolate biscuits along, just for you."

Lucinda placed the tin on the table. It was red, with a special pattern on the lid and Duchess knew they were the best chocolate biscuits in the land.

Miss Pillinger continued, "Teeny Tiny Witch, we welcome you home. I have heard all about your adventures on the wizard's island. You have earned the right to return to the academy and complete your training after the summer holiday - if you want to?"

Miss Pillinger took Teeny Tiny Witch's hand and shook it, and then handed her a certificate.

"Your 1st year examination, passed with honours."

Teeny Tiny Witch grinned as Miss Pillinger continued, "If the icy witch queen returns, she will not be in power, for we have a new queen in mind. Will you come back to the academy — please?"

Teeny Tiny Witch was speechless but she nodded. Her cheeks were as red as her pointy hat and her red cloak and shoes.

Miss Pillinger then turned to Teeny Tiny Witch's mother. "Mother Pearl, it is my honour to announce, by vote of everyone here at Witch Island, that you are the one we want for our new queen. Will you accept the position and go to live in the castle?"

Miss Pillinger snapped her fingers and a purple velvet cushion appeared. On it rested the diamond encrusted silver and gold crown of the witches. It had the phases of the moon all the way around it and a full moon right in front, with a moonstone, as big as a peppermint, set in its centre. The beautiful crown was rarely seen as it was worn only for the most important ceremonies.

Everyone turned to Mother Pearl, waiting to hear what she would say.

Mother Pearl smiled proudly. Duchess smiled. Lucinda and Henry smiled, too. But the biggest smile of all belonged to

Teeny Tiny Witch. She could barely keep from jumping up and down and yelling in delight.

"I would be honoured; yes, thank you." said Mother Pearl, graciously.

Miss Pillinger placed the crown upon her head, saying, "Then long may you rule, with kindness, understanding and mercy."

"I shall do my best," Queen Mother Pearl said, seriously.

Everyone cheered so loudly that it made Teeny Tiny Witch jump. That's when she noticed that all the young witches, the other teachers, and even Ned-Ted, the two-headed python, had clustered around, observing the ceremony.

It was very crowded in the small cottage, but everyone was so happy that they hardly noticed.

"How good it is to be home," said Teeny Tiny Witch as she hugged her mother joyfully. "Oh, Mother, does this make me a princess witch?"

"Yes, Princess Teeny Tiny Witch," said the new queen.

Miss Pillinger added, "Indeed, and our first ever, because none of the other queens had children."

"Oh, my, and now George can return, without having to carry me back. I know he will be glad of that." Everyone laughed, because they knew how George complained of his aching back.

Queen Mother Pearl said, "My first act as queen is to retire George to a life of ease. He will never have to carry anyone again, and we will just enjoy his wise advice and funny ways.

"Thank you, Mother. George is a bit grumpy but he's fun to be with," Teeny Tiny Witch said, fondly.

"That is exactly why I sent him with you, darling. George was my very first broom, and yours too. He is a very special broom."

"How sweet," said Miss Pillinger. "Yes, it's true. We witches can't do without our brooms."

As everyone left, they all said how grateful they were to Teeny Tiny Witch, and thanked Queen Mother Pearl for accepting the position as Queen of Witch Island, saying, "It's nicer to have a Mother Pearl for our queen than an icy one."

"Yes, and when the news reaches all the sea-creatures, I am sure they will return to the Magic Sea," said Ned-Ted.

12

The Wizard's Wand

When everyone else had left, Miss Pillinger, Lucinda and Teeny Tiny Witch sat with Queen Mother Pearl in the cottage. Duchess followed the conversation through the window.

Teeny Tiny Witch said, "Mother, the wizard is very upset because he can't find his wand, and he thinks he has lost his powers. I want to find his wand so he will be happy again, as he was when he got new glasses."

"Of course," said her mother, "but where could it be?"

Miss Pillinger said, "The icy witch queen used to live in the castle; she might have hidden it somewhere inside. It's your castle now, so I would start by searching there." She stood up. "Now I must be off; so much to do before the start of the next term, you know."

Lucinda stayed behind. "I want to help search," she said.

"Thank you, Lucinda; you are a very good friend," said Teeny Tiny Witch. "Maybe one day I will learn the spell to turn your green skin back to its normal colour."

"Please don't; I've got used to it now," said Lucinda. "Like your red cloak and hat, it makes me different. I feel special and I have you to thank for it. Plus, frogs are cute," she grinned.

Queen Mother Pearl said, "Duchess, before you go home, please would you come to the castle and help us search?"

"It will be my pleasure," said Duchess. I'll even take you there!" She allowed everyone to climb on her back. "Hold tight!" she called out.

"Wow!" they gasped as, with a few beats of her enormous wings, Duchess carried them up, up into the air.

Before long they reached the castle, which rose high above everything else on the island. It looked as dark and bleak as ever.

"This place gives me the creeps," said Duchess, as she landed in the courtyard. A huge brass-bound oak door led into the wing where the icy witch queen had lived.

Queen Mother Pearl said, "I am glad I came, for since we are moving in tomorrow, it is a good idea to have a thorough look at the place."

They entered the castle, which was bitterly cold. The stone walls and floor, and the high ceilings, only added to the icy feel of the place.

"The wizard often told me how uncomfortable he felt when he visited his cousin. Now I understand why she was known as the icy witch queen; even I would find it difficult to be pleasant living in a castle as cold as this," said Queen Mother Pearl.

Duchess hurried to the huge fireplace where there was a pile of unburned logs. Taking a deep breath, she blew flames over them until they were glowing with rosy red embers. As the fire started to burn it filled the air with the rich scent of wood smoke. The flickering flames gave off plenty of warmth and light.

Queen Mother Pearl thanked the helpful dragon, and Teeny Tiny Witch said, "It's not so gloomy anymore. It feels quite cheerful."

"Yes, it does," Lucinda agreed. "See how different everything looks. Why, those stones in the wall are pink! Oh, it looks so pretty now!"

Duchess said, "The castle knows it has new owners and it is positively glowing pink with happiness. It is because Queen Mother Pearl has such a kind and cheerful personality."

"Oh, hush now, you'll have me blushing," Mother Pearl said, shyly lowering her rosy face.

"Oh, Mother, it is true. The castle is delighted to have you."

"Delighted to have *us*, daughter," Queen Mother Pearl said, regaining her composure. She laughed, and everyone joined in. Their laughter echoed around them cheerfully, as though the castle laughed, too. Clearly it was happy with its new residents.

Now they felt ready to tackle the search for the wizard's wand. They were all confident that it must be close by and Teeny Tiny Witch was sure they would find it within minutes.

They looked high and low, peering into every nook and cranny, and even discovered some hidden passages in their search. The passages were dusty and occupied by mice and huge spiders, which sent Lucinda and Teeny Tiny Witch hurrying by as fast as they could, trying not to scream.

They looked in the cupboards, but found nothing.

They looked on the table, and found nothing.

They even looked under the icy witch queen's old bed, and still turned up nothing.

"It can't be here," said Duchess. "There's nowhere else to look."

Queen Mother Pearl said, "I think it is right under our noses and we are searching too hard. Knowing Miranda, she would hide it somewhere really obvious, where we have not thought of looking."

They carried on searching, looking in lamp shades and under cushions. Duchess thumped the thick tapestry wall hangings with her tail, but only succeeded in showering herself – and everyone else - with dust. When they had all stopped coughing, she said, "I don't think it is here. I'll stop now."

"Thank you, Duchess," the others said, wiping tears from their red-rimmed eyes.

And that's when Queen Mother Pearl, blinking the dust out of her eyes, noticed the painting. It was on a wall by the bed in the icy witch queen's old bedroom. The picture was of a wizard and his wand! She gasped, and everyone gathered round to see. The wizard in the painting looked exactly like *their* wizard!

"Mother, is this a portrait that Miranda made of her cousin?" asked Teeny Tiny Witch. "The resemblance is amazing."

"That wand does look just like the stolen one," said Duchess. "I didn't know Miranda was such a good artist."

"Wait a minute. That isn't a painted wand; it's the real one!" Lucinda exclaimed. "It's held to the painting by a powerful spell."

"What should we do?" Teeny Tiny Witch asked. "It won't come undone."

"Of course it will," said Duchess. "Stand back and let me try something. Don't worry; no fire, I promise."

Duchess snapped her sharp teeth at the wand, trying to pull it from the picture, but that didn't work. It was set firm within the canvas and would not come loose.

Teeny Tiny Witch tried to magic it down. That didn't work either.

Lucinda tried to pull it off with her fingers, while chanting a loosening spell, but its magic bound it tight. Without the correct spell, the wand stayed part of the painting.

Duchess said, "I could take the painting to the wizard. Maybe the sight of it would give him back enough strength to free the wand."

"I'd like to try first," Queen Mother Pearl said, "but I must ask that you all go outside while I perform my spell; it could be dangerous and I don't want anyone hurt."

They obeyed, and went to wait in the corridor, closing the door firmly behind them.

Moments later, Teeny Tiny Witch heard something she had never heard before. Mother was chanting spells in a very strange language. Her voice got higher and higher, until she was almost shouting. Then they heard a terrible scream, followed by a crash.

Teeny Tiny Witch glanced at the others, worried, then breathed a sigh of relief as she heard her mother's voice, sounding perfectly normal once more.

"You can come in, now."

As the door opened, they saw Queen Mother Pearl proudly holding the wand. It shone beautifully.

"Oh, well done," said Duchess. "But how did you manage it?"

"A secret spell; something I remember from long, long ago," the queen replied.

Teeny Tiny Witch spotted something on the floor. A small piece of the wand had broken off when it fell. She picked it up and put it safely into her cloak pocket. 'Perhaps,' she thought, 'this will help my spells to work in future!'

Everyone was happy, for now the wizard would get his wand back and would soon be his old, cheerful self.

Duchess agreed to return the wand, before bringing George back to the castle. "I need to get back to see Quanga anyway," she said. "The wizard will be so happy," she added, "that he might even throw another party; hopefully, one without naughty magic cakes."

This time it was Teeny Tiny Witch who blushed, as they all waved goodbye to Duchess.

"I miss Quanga and George," said the little witch, "but it's so good to have you as my friend, Lucinda."

Mother put her arm around Teeny Tiny Witch and Lucinda and gave them both a big hug. They hugged her back and Lucinda's smile grew as wide as a frog's.

"Do you know, I think there might be some chocolate biscuits left?" said Queen Mother Pearl. She waved her hand and the red tin of biscuits appeared.

"It's good to be home," Teeny Tiny Witch sighed. "Really good."

THE END

Also from Blue Poppy Publishing

For Cats' Eyes Only – By Olli Tooley
Illustrated by Amii James

Special Agent Felix Whiter always gets his man... or tortoise.

Or does he? Sometimes the tortoise gives him the slip, and sometimes the real villain is... oh but that would be telling.

A very silly spy thriller for kids, with plenty of giggles for adults too. "For Cats' Eyes Only" is packed with excitement, danger, terrible puns, and fart humour.

Educational allergy advice.

This is intended to be a purely FUN story and every effort has been made to remove all traces of education and morality from it, however it has been produced in an environment where educational elements are included in other books, and as such the publisher cannot be held liable should you inadvertently learn anything by reading this book.

For Cats' Eyes Only

Special Agent Felix Whiter always gets his man... or tortoise.

Or does he? Sometimes the tortoise gives him the slip, and sometimes the real villain is... oh but that would be telling.

A fun, if sometimes silly, spy thriller for kids, with plenty of giggles for adults too. "For Cats' Eyes Only" is packed with excitement, danger, terrible puns, and fart humour.

Educational allergy advice

This is intended to be a purely [...] and every effort has been mad[...] all traces of education and use[...] it, however it has been [...] environment where education[...] are included in other books [...] the publisher cannot be held [...] you inadvertently learn a[...] reading this book.

BLUE POPPY PUBLISHING
ISBN 978-1-91[...]
9 781911[...]

For Cats' Eyes Only

Olli Tooley
Amii James

About Sheila Golding

Sheila Golding was born in Tiverton, Devon and educated at Tiverton Grammar School. She spent much of her working life with the NHS, as well as bringing up her six children.

Sheila first discovered her love of writing in 2009, spending her spare time writing poetry, a few of her poems being published over the years, and developing the love of writing children's stories.

Sheila now lives in Ilfracombe, and enjoys walking coastal paths, sharing her writing with others, and spending time with her six children, eight grandchildren, and two dogs.

Sheila is extremely excited about her first children's story being published, saying, 'It is a dream come true'.